Issue 1

Issue 1

Publisher
Tower Ravens, LLC

Editor in Chief
Michael Sorenson

Editorial Contributors
Mark Wilkinson, Kristen Redd Wilkinson, Michael Sorenson, Laura Sorenson

Artistic Contributors
Michael Sorenson, Eric Wallis

Speculative Fiction Illustrated is published semi-annually in print and digital formats.

ISSN: 2993-7566 (print), 2995-7850 (digital)

ISBN: 978-1-966681-00-7 (print), 978-1-966681-01-4 (digital)

Advertising inquiries: Contact Tower Ravens via post (address below).

Submissions: SFI has an open submissions policy. For more information, refer to the SFI website (URL below).

Obverse Cover: "Autumn Quest," by Michael Sorenson

Reverse Cover: "Rubik's Cubes," by Michael Sorenson

Text: SFI uses Impact font designed by Geoffrey Lee for title text, and Palatino Linotype font by Hermann Zapf for body text.

© 2023, Tower Ravens, LLC. All rights reserved. No part of this publication shall be reproduced, stored in a retrieval system, or transmitted by any means, electronic, mechanical, psychic, photographic, photostatic, audible, performance, or otherwise—nor used in the development, training, testing, or other aspects of artificial intelligence, or other analytical models—without the written permission of the publisher. Reprint inquiries may be made to Tower Ravens, LLC, via post (address below).

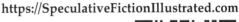

https://SpeculativeFictionIllustrated.com

Tower Ravens, LLC
1780 E 1850 North
North Logan, UT 84341
USA

Contents

EDITORS' WELCOME

vii

BLUE STARLIGHT

Mark Wilkinson

1

RUBIK'S CUBES

K. R. Wilkinson

15

THE WIND AND THE WATER

M. C. Sorenson

19

Editor's Welcome

Michael Sorenson

Welcome to the first issue of Speculative Fiction Illustrated, the magazine that's just for you!

For me, you ask?

Yes, for you.

Well, then, what is Speculative Fiction Illustrated?

Speculative Fiction Illustrated, or SFI for short, is a magazine that is dedicated to showcasing creative works by amateur writers and artists. Why amateurs? Because, while many writers and artists function in a professional capacity by publishing novels, or working in the illustration industry, many people create simply because they enjoy it. Maybe it's a hobby, maybe it's a late-in-life career change, maybe it's a desire to develop a talent that has been lying dormant and waiting for the right impetus to begin. Whatever it might be, we believe that there should be an opportunity for them, to share with you, what they are ready to create.

So, what is speculative fiction?

Speculative fiction is a step outside of reality. Sometimes it's a big step, ranging from a slight twisting of the real world, to the full blown creation of new worlds populated with wonderful new creatures and people. It includes, but isn't limited to, science fiction, fantasy, surrealism, horror, science fantasy, space opera, alternate history and magical realism.

Why speculative fiction?

The short answer: it's fun!

The not so short answer: speculative fiction gives writers and artists the ability to share their thoughts, feelings, and beliefs through characters they create within a framework that is free of the limitation of mainstream realism. It also allows for flights of imagination that would not be available otherwise. It makes the seemingly ridiculous look real, but with the added dimension of exploring the human condition

It also allows for the writer and artist to develop ideas that aren't bound by the constraints of the modern world; nor dictated by the ever changing social order.

What more is there?

Lots. First, there's the goal that every story and picture included in the magazine will withstand the test of time. In essence, it becomes a classic, going beyond the current, or soon to be outdated mores and opinions that shift from day to day, and year to year.

Second, the dedicated copy that you are now holding in your hands. Whether you've purchased an ebook, or a hard copy print volume, it is meant for leisure reading in the quiet solitude of your own life and away from the distractions of the outside world.

Third, a variety of styles, themes, attitudes and philosophies wrapped up in stories and art that range from the serious and familiar to the strange and funny.

Lastly, we believe that writing and art can be entertaining, as well as compelling, without the more degrading hallmarks of modern fiction. We believe that emotion and conflict can be conveyed without the passive/aggressive shorthand of profanity. We believe in the sanctity of sexuality between husband and wife, and not the blatant and gratuitous imagery of pornography, either visual or written. We believe that while violence is a part of adventure fiction, it need not be extravagant, nor grotesque. We also believe in the respect of one's beliefs, and find that the institutional cleansing of religious thought from not only speculative fiction, but from all fiction to be offensive.

In short, Speculative Fiction Illustrated is created not only as a means to explore imaginary worlds and celebrate the talents of others, but also as a mental landing pad, where one can touch down, decompress, and refuel.

I hope you enjoy, Speculative Fiction Illustrated.

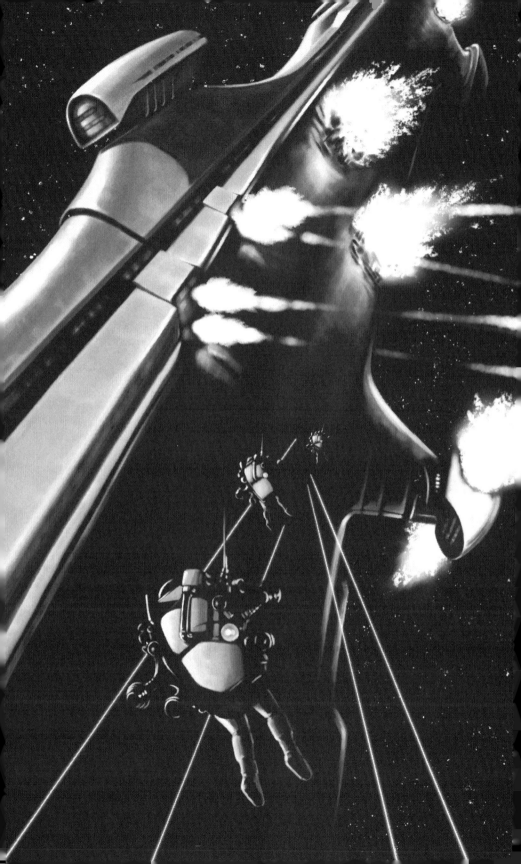

BLUE STARLIGHT

MARK WILKINSON

The mayhem of the battlefield is so different in space. It lacks everything of the human experience—acrid smoke, red-hot flames, thundering cannons, scorched earth—everything except sight and death. Even in the newsreels, they alter what is real to make a scene viewers will watch.

In the visor of my spacesuit, the ranging radar ticks down both time and distance. Ahead the looming spaceship grows larger in my eyes. It looks so unreal. Where blue starlight strikes the hull, the glare is brilliant. Where the shadows fall, the blackness is as dark as space. The break between darkness and light is sharp.

Explosions flash before me and about me as kinetic shells pound our target. Behind me, I know the scene is the same on the hull of the ship that brought me here, my home of three years. Thin beams of laser fire snap all about me. At any instant, my battle could end. Their flash is so sudden and so perfectly straight that it is impossible to tell which end is the origin and which is the target.

Yet despite the vivid images before me, this, like the half-dozen other battles I survived, is unreal. Were it not for the mortal fear in my heart, I would believe it a dream. It has no sound, and the colors are all wrong.

The horrendous explosions against the hull of our target do nothing to deafen me. There isn't even so much as the clang of metal-on-metal. And the reflected light of the blue star lacks all the yellow warmth of a living one.

As the distance closes, only two sounds enter my ears. I can hear my own breathing, which is loud against the faceplate of my armored spacesuit. And I can hear the orders of Major Toonel coming over the comm, seeking calm in chaos as troops are led to the enemy hull or through death's door.

The whole scene reminds me of the tactical reviews that Colonel Rennis gave every-other Thursday in the academy's dining hall. Though military in content, their intent was to entertain, and they were one of the highlights of my academic years. I would endure the razing of my classmates to sit toward the front where I could clearly see every facet of the muted battle footage.

Colonel Rennis was retired, an old man, with a fallen stature and a broken voice. One could see the former immensity of his frame, but I always wondered if his voice ever boomed with command authority. It was the combination of the tinny microphone, his heavy breathing, his monotone dialogue, and the silent video on the huge screen that reminded me of these deep space battlefields.

I know that the predictability of our battlefield tactics will someday betray us. As my range meter clicks from 1001 meters to 1000 meters, the kinetic bombardment against our target ceases. My 8 men and I lead point on this assault, the forlorn hope. Now our enemy knows I am less than 10 seconds from impacting their world, 14 seconds from being fully lethal.

At 7 seconds from impact, a computer in my ranging radar sends an imperceptible tickle to the command computer of my thrust pack. With the jolt of an emergency stop, I am pressed forward in my spacesuit. Through my back, I can feel the rumbling thrusters. Ahead, my target slows. Its cold blue-black surface is uninviting, but it looks placid compared with the apocalyptic visage we place on the scene. Hostile or not, it would be violently invaded.

I bring my knees forward, with my ankles straight and my feet pointed down. Under the armor, I am still human, still naked. Elbows out, hands up, palms in, and I clench my fists, toes, and teeth for good measure. It is a drill I can do badly wounded and on the verge of consciousness—I am not that lucky this time.

The suffocating deceleration of the thrust pack ends as abruptly as it began. All the buckles and belts restraining my armored body within its steel cradle pop in unison. No rumbling fills my bones. I am weightless and falling. My own breathing becomes amplified, quick and shallow as it echoes in my helmet. The Colonel Rennis-like voice drawls on about red and blue arrows cresting the green hills of the Vergugo Crest on treads of grey. The screen fills me with horror.

The bland, featureless hull gives no indication of its range from me. The thrust pack carried the ranging radar away. My impact is unexpected, hard, and all too familiar. Ironically, I am safer here. I welcome the hard impact. It means a faster arrival, less time hanging in empty space like a carnival duck against a black canvas backdrop.

The powerful magnets on my knees and on the backs of my hands hold me fast. The autonomy of my training continues. I release all the magnets but the one on my right hand. As I flip around from kneeling to my back, I draw my rifle from over my left shoulder. Being left-handed caused me no end of trouble with the drill instructors. As my feet swing around, they plant firmly on the starship hull, their magnets latching.

I hang there on the side of this foreign starship looking out into space. I feel as though it is night, and I stand on the ledge of a skyscraper. I can almost feel the night air blowing through my helmet. The stars became offices on adjacent buildings—accountants finishing inventories, engineers completing charts, lawyers sweating over the fate of their clients. On the street below, they become streetlights, taxies, and buses.

The magnet on my right hand releases, and I pitch forward, leaning to the street below, as if to throw myself from the skyscraper. I want to fall, to carry the aches and agonies of my soul down to one bright flash of pain, of death. Only the stars' lack of symmetry, their complete randomness, dispels my vision. Instead of falling, I find myself standing upright on the hull of my enemy's starship. I steady the barrel of my weapon with my right hand and survey the scene.

I can see a few of my men recovering about me. The damage on the starship is lighter than expected; still, there is the usual amount of debris tumbling about. We dropped much further aft than I expected. A hull traverse is dangerous and entry time with the lighter damage will be longer. The casualties would be high.

"Point team, aft objective, rendezvous keel mark." My men know we are in a bad situation for me to make this call. To prevent a siege scenario from developing, bombardment will begin again, and we'll have to contend with hull shudder and shrapnel. I begin plodding along in my magnetic boots. Sure enough, I have to increase the stick as the ground begins buckling below me. No time had been wasted renewing the bombardment.

Fortunately, luck is with us. Heightened above the droning battle coordination comes the voice of one of my men, "Captain Wexel, there's a flexure tear. Um, Herod's turret, bow 20, keel 10." I can hear enthusiasm mixed with fear in his voice. I hope, beyond reason, that his find will improve our situation. Still, the tear is only 20 meters forward of and 10 meters below the ship's anti-personnel turret—a turret which could no longer be brought to bear against us. It isn't far off course. I change the order.

Locating the tear in the hull was lucky. Unfortunately, it is very unlikely it will pan out for us. Such long-range deep spacecraft like this require enormous fuel supplies. Indeed, more than half a destroyer's volume is fuel. When structural buckling causes a tear in the hull, it generally occurs around the fuel tanks.

This isn't because fuel occupies so much of a starship's space. Starship fuel is highly reactive, but it isn't very explosive. It takes careful manipulation to cause the fuel to undergo fusion and provide propulsion. Neither a laser cannon blast nor a kinetic shell explosion will cause the fuel to combust. Fuel is practically armor. Fuel tanks are often placed against the outer hull.

For shock, however, fuel tanks are horrible. A long cylindrical shell, hollowed out for liquid fuel, is bad in combat. A full tank will carry the shock of an explosion through its entire length and down into the inner hull of a ship, shocking the whole ship violently. An empty tank is even worse. Instead of the shock traveling through the tank, it ripples along the skin, like a pebble striking water. When the explosions' ripple hits the stiff end of the tank, it reflects back and travels along the tank's length a second, third, even fourth time.

I think about this as I march to the tear. Bits of shrapnel seem to appear for nowhere as they cross the inky blackness of shadows and suddenly appear as starlight strikes them. They are too clandestine and quick to dodge. I could die at any moment. The march keeps the terror from my mind.

A starship's superstructure is designed to flex against forces and dampen vibrations. It is designed to hold together all the pieces of the starship as they move about under the accelerations of travel and the pounding of combat.

Because fuel tanks don't flex and don't dampen vibrations, they buckle and tear. While I plod along the shaking hull, I don't expect to find entry to the ship's interior. I expect to find the starship's metal hull torn, gaping open just far enough to tempt entry, and closed enough to threaten a torn spacesuit.

But I know I won't be tempted. I know what I will find. Inside the tear, I'll see a fuel tank that had been beat to uselessness. Its outer composite shell will be badly wrinkled with fractures like cracked glass. Forcing itself out of the fractures and drifting out of the starship will be bits of insulation—bits of insulation broken, ground, and ejected by the violent shaking of the tank's inner body. And if the shaking had been sufficiently violent, the tank itself will be split open, revealing globs of fuel.

The tear found by my crew will be an entry to the most dangerous place within the starship. A cryogenic ball of slush would likely meet a soldier entering a fuel tank. Like the vacuum of space pulls air from a man's chest, or tears his lungs open trying, fuel slush sucks warmth from a man's core.

Such a death would stop a man's heart in half a gasp. I would welcome such a death when offered next to drowning. How does a soldier drown in space? When a laser cuts through a spacesuit, a gummy inner layer of adhesive almost instantly seals the hole it makes. This prevents suffocation and decompression illness. But if the laser shot hits the suit's liquid heating and cooling system, the skin-tight combat spacesuit can fill with liquid paraffin before the life support system can shut it down. In space assault school, they don't tell you how many ways there are to die. Not enough time, I suppose.

Finally, I arrive at the split in the hull. One of my men arrives at the same time as me. Jackson, Maxley, and Pratt already stand around the split.

"Maxley, don't straddle the tear," I shout at one of the younger men on my crew. He hurriedly side steps. "Roll call," I tell the throat-mike. Jack Harrison, walking up with me, knows I'm talking to him. He begins replying as I stomp to the tear's edge.

"We lost communication with Abernathy and Morris during descent," he started. If I lived, I'll have to write letters to their mothers, telling them how they died bravely defending the republic from the evil military oligarchy. I'm tired of writing those letters. It takes so long to follow the tradition of using ink and parchment.

Looking down the fissure into the starship, I don't see what I expected.

Harrison continues, "Rosen had a mechanical failure." I feel my heart stop—my friend. Tears fill my eyes. "He didn't make the landing and is counting stars." I blink the tears away and gain control of myself. I am horrified—no, mystified—that such an emotion can still well up within me. "He said he'd name one after your daughter." Lucky fool. I almost kick off the hull to join him in the heavens.

End caps. Through the broken insulation, I look down at the gap between fuel tanks. I am looking at two fuel tank end caps. We are in luck. I might live through this after all.

"Vickers went silent a few moments ago," Harrison was wrapping up. I mouth the words with him, "All present or accounted for, sir."

Though three of my men are dead, I am overjoyed with this find. "Pratt, great work!" I say it with elation in my voice. We have an avenue to the inner hull, and my friend Rosen has taken up stellar cartography. I think I'll take up stellar cartography when this is all over. Time for action.

"Jackson, Maxley, down the hole fast," I gesture down the hole with my finger. "If that sucker pinches before you're through, we'll only have half of you to bury." Though they are already moving quickly, I give them a little encouragement, "MOVE IT!

"Pratt and Harrison, bring up the rear," I say as I stare intently at the gap in the hull. In weightlessness, you cannot jump down a hole. You can jump up one, but it takes gravity to do anything down. Once again, the world around me changes. The ergonomics of this spacesuit amaze me. I bend at the waist and grab the lip of the hull's tear with my right hand. My left hand clutches the grip of my rifle. I hold the rifle steady by gripping the stock with my underarm.

I stand, bent over, looking at the two pairs of feet falling before me. I wish someone would yell at me, tell me to get down the hole. I release both magnets, and my feet swing upward—or downward?

I hang like a drop of blood from this starship's laceration. If I could, I would let go and plummet through eternity naming stars for all the people I met in life. Instead, I pull myself into the tear and infest the steel organism.

I leave a world where mindless shells fall from space to shake the ground below. The danger of their impersonal bombardment is replaced by the danger of marines guarding their sovereign territory. The new attacks would be intentional and surgical.

The moment of breaching the hull is, for me, the most terrifying phase of a mission. The fanciful realm of space, with its blue stars, razor-sharp shadows, and directionless emptiness passes like a curtain. I enter a world with yellow lights, structural patterns, and tight corridors. It terrifies me.

I focus on the feet before me. They are driven by command, my command. I can remember being the feet. It was much easier. Now I understand why the commander doesn't go first. It isn't to protect him from the trap or even the first shot. He obeys not the command of a superior, but the command of his will. And no mans' will is strong enough to blindly crawl into the maw of a predator for a conviction which eludes him.

They obey my command, so they go and drag my broken will behind them.

As I descend into the spacecraft, my fear subsides. I find that I am between the two fuel tank end caps. I'm falling down a gangway, and my mind reorients itself again.

We entered a tear in the port side of the starship. One of the end caps is part of a fuel tank that travels toward the bow of the starship. The other is the end of a fuel tank that travels to the aft. Mast-side and keel-side, above and below, more tanks parallel these two.

I turn myself, swinging my feet to the new down, and I stick my magnetic boots to the gangway. Behind me, my two men do the same. Ahead, the others drift to the starship's inner hull before righting themselves.

We find ourselves at a maintenance hatch. This is much better than an inner hatch or an airlock hatch, both of which would have indicators on the bridge. The only catch was decompression. An inner hatch closes off hatchways between bulkheads. Bulkheads separate sections of the ship. If one section unexpectedly decompresses, inner hatches prevent additional sections from losing pressure. An airlock is, of course, a small passageway that can be easily pressurized or depressurized to allow passage from a hard vacuum to a livable section of the ship.

A maintenance hatch is altogether different. It normally separates a decompressed section of the ship from a livable section of the ship. Maintenance hatches are only opened when an entire section of the ship is depressurized for engineering maintenance. It is perfect for us.

"Pratt," I point at the door, "check it." He steps forward, slinging his rifle. He draws out a small cutting torch. My heart is pounding hard. The reality of our situation is again getting to me. We are about to engage in close-quarters combat. In a moment, I'll be trying to kill people before they kill me.

"Captain," Pratt's voice snaps me back to the situation, "residual pressure only."

"Gimmie a pet door," I reply. Time is of the essence. If we are discovered before we get through, entry will be extremely costly. Pratt will cut a hole large enough for shoulders and a life support pack, and no more.

As I expected, the enemy starship had depressurized before they approached our ship under a diplomacy standard. There was no mistake in protocol. They intended from the first moment to open fire on us. Because of the damage that explosive depressurization can cause, not only to humans but also to starship systems, it is standard procedure to suit up and depressurize a ship before engaging in combat.

Our boarding teams were half-staffed, because we were not on full alert, which is why I'm here with so few men. Twenty seconds after they fired their surprise volley, I was hurled toward them at a very unsafe speed.

"Five seconds!" Pratt hollers, his helmet buried in the glow of the cutting torch.

There was only one way to quell my uneasy stomach, and that was to get into the action. "Jackson, Maxley, send me through, battering ram style," I order. My left hand is still affixed to the grip of my rifle. That hadn't changed since I landed, and it isn't about to change now. I hold the barrel against my chest as Maxley grabs my right arm and Jackson grabs my left. I detach my boots, and they lay me on the ground.

"Clear!" Pratt is almost panicky in his tone of voice. He worries me. Still, he is really good with a cutting torch. I wouldn't want to be here without him.

Jackson and Maxley shove me through the hole. I'm on my back looking at the ceiling. As I pass through the hole in the hatch, I use my periphery vision only. I take in everything at once. I fire off four volleys from my laser rifle before my right shoulder hits the wall.

Movement in zero-g is a terrible thing. If you try to smack someone on top of the head with a club, your own body pitches backward. You're lucky if you don't hit yourself in the groin. If you swing a rifle rapidly to bear on a target, your torso swings the opposite direction. If your feet are not planted, like mine aren't now, you're at the mercy of inertia.

As I passed through Pratt's dog door, I saw a spacesuit-clad figure in the corridor to my right, the bow-ward direction of the starship. From my shoulder to my right side, I rotated my rifle close to my body's center of mass. I turned ever so slightly as I fired. Three of the four shots struck my target, and then my right shoulder bounced against the wall opposite our dog door.

As I bounce back to the makeshift door, my left boot clips Jackson's helmet. He hardly seems to notice, his rifle already trained on my target. I manage to get a boot on the wall, then another. I stand on the wall, covering my men as they crawl carefully through the improvised doorway. The target doesn't move. After Jackson gets all the way through, I begin advancing.

My opponent is a spacesuit clad individual. One foot is planted on the deck, the other is detached with its toes loosely touching, as if he were about to walk backward. The target's body is slumped into the fetal position, knees bent, arms tucked in, and body folded forward. It would be an impossible balancing act if there were any gravity at all.

The opponent's spacesuit is what we call construction quality. It has small plastic plates impregnated into the mesh of the suit's outer fabric. It's designed to protect against tool mishap, not against the blast of a laser rifle. He must be a tech worker.

Jackson approaches the target and holds his position. I'm already shouldering my rifle. In all the missions I've performed, having boarded ships as small as a private yacht and one really big military cruiser, my hand has never before been so far from my trigger.

In my younger years, I bragged about executing smugglers in interstellar space. I wore my medals proudly. The pride is gone, but the medals remain. I actually flaunt these atrocities every time we pull into port. The bright ribbons on the dull grey dress uniform mark me as some type of war hero. To me, good or bad, it means I'm a killer, and people praise me for it.

"Get this man a dose of metastil," I shout at my men. There is a look of shock on their faces, but they obey. Harrison steps forward, brandishes the long, heavy gauge needle. I grab my victim and raise his arm. His magnetic boot pops loose. Jackson steps forward to cover us as Maxley lets his rifle go to help me steady the dying young man. I manage to raise his arm, and Harrison works the long needle through the finer fabric of the armpit and into the man's flesh. Harrison injects the drug into the man's system.

His open eyes, the blank pupils, the mouth agape in horror show me a being struggling to hold together an infinitely precious aura that I alone tore asunder. As the drug courses through this broken soul, the pupils roll into the man's skull, his eyes still open. The horror on his mouth goes slack.

Maxley tentatively releases the man's legs and recovers his weapon from the space where he left it. I alone cradle the broken man, now sleeping, whether to death or life nobody would know until his suit could be stripped from him.

The thundering vibrations through the starship begin to subside. The superstructure dampens them, and no further shelling renews the shuddering. Outside, they realized what I realized: There'd be no contest of arms here. The battle ends, and I weep.

• • •

I drop the feather quill on the brown parchment. I stand. In our assault, we faced no marines and only a skeleton crew. It had been a last ditch effort by a defeated people, a mere show of defiance. I wipe the stale sweat from my fingers against the legs of my jumpsuit. I grab the parchment from the small desk in my cramped quarters and read it aloud to myself.

"Dear Madam Abernathy.

"A grateful nation accepted the sacrifice of your son, Charles Dale Abernathy, in the battle of Omega Thuve. As is the military tradition, your son was interred in space about Omega Thuve's orbit. A representative of my unit will contact you shortly to arrange your son's memorial. By tradition, these services will be conducted as Omega Thuve passes over the longitude of his hometown.

"I commanded your son in this fatal battle and in two battles prior. I do not hesitate to nominate him to the Order of the Hall of the Heavens and have done so. A plaque commemorating this appointment will be awarded to you at your son's memorial.

"Let me share with you the circumstances surrounding your son's death.

"Under a flag of diplomacy the enemy destroyer Osephus approached our starship, the Indestructible. Your son and I were on regular rotation, as a battle alert had not been sounded. When the Osephus began shelling us unexpectedly, I was deployed with a detachment of eight men to board and cripple the starship.

"Your son assaulted the starship at my side through an opening created by battle damage, a hull tear between the destroyer's fuel tanks. We lost several men during this boarding operation as we were heavily outnumbered and outgunned by enemy marines. While fighting to enter the destroyer, your son was injured. Nevertheless, he assured me his wound was not severe and accompanied me as we traversed the destroyer's interior and ultimately assaulted the remaining contingent of enemy marines on the bridge.

"Though your son received no additional injuries, he collapsed on the bridge because of his prior wound. I did not see the moment when he fell. The intensity of the fighting, I regret to inform you, prevented him from leaving any parting words.

"I am saddened this letter is all I can give to ease the pain of your loss. Do not ever hesitate to share your son's valor, and his story, with those that did not know him.

"Sincerely, Captain Darius Wexel.

Tired of the lies, I slap the parchment down on my desk. I stare at the orders next to it: a new assignment to a new war.

Alien Landscape, Eric Wallis. Illustration for Universe, The Sci-Fi RPG published by Tower Ravens, LLC.

Rubik's Cubes

K. R. Wilkinson

No one would've thought our sleepy Los Angeles suburb would be the place where news of aliens broke. I mean, our biggest annual excitement was watching the fire trucks extinguish fresh flames on the hills started by the city's own 4th of July fireworks show.

But we also had Emily Christensen. Emily wasn't that remarkable to a national audience, but she was kind of famous at our school for skipping a grade. And for the Rubik's Cubes. Ever since these "toys" hit the shelves, they'd just become increasingly cool. After Christmas that year, it seemed like everyone on the campus had at least one, but usually three or more. And after wearing their earrings as checkerboards, or making their keychains into snake eyes, kids would always end up messing them up. Emily was the only one we knew who could put them right.

It got out of hand pretty quickly. Every lunchtime kids lined up for a turn to get their cubes solved. Everyone knew that if you removed the stickers or took them apart they were never really the same again. Emily probably could have charged a quarter a cube and had her own little racket going, but I think she solved them just for the challenge. I finally had to put my foot down and limit her "customers" to only the second half of each lunch period. I missed my friend, you know?

But I guess there were an unusual number of Rubik's Cubes getting solved at our middle school, and it drew attention. You have to remember, this was before everyone was carrying around a computer in their pocket. The best entertainment we had was a local arcade where we would spend the afternoon feeding quarters into a machine as fast as Pac-Man ate dots. Or if our parents had enough money, we could zap the flying saucers of Space Invaders on our Atari 2600. We never dreamt there could be technology embedded in the Rubik's Cubes monitoring their moves—and ours.

And who would do such a thing anyway? The bad guys of our day were the Russians, and what we feared was that everyone would launch their nukes and annihilate each other. Talk of UFOs and aliens was just a joke about "little green men" and Area 51. The real aliens were much more subtle. I mean, who would have thought Ernö Rubik wasn't just an eccentric genius, but actually from another planet? One who's technology was waaaay beyond ours?

We might have stayed oblivious too, if it weren't for Patty Jo Packer. Patty Jo, well, she was not from California. She brought to our school every stereotype of a southern gossip. She had the accent, the big hair, and she loved to get the scoop on everything going on. It was Patty Jo who asked around and found out that pretty much everyone in the school had received an invitation in the mail to join an exclusive puzzle-solving club. But how exclusive could it be if we were all invited?

Patty Jo was also the first one to notice the men in dark suits hanging around and to point them out to us all. They didn't come onto the school grounds, but we started to spot them everywhere around town, watching us.

Of course, Jason Stone told his parents. We were all enjoying the intrigue, but Jason always played by the rules. Jason told his dad, his dad told the police, and the police made arrests. Then the whole government descended on our town.

The dark-suited men who were arrested had sketchy backgrounds and vague government ID. They demanded release, but our police chief wouldn't budge. He was protecting the kids, he said. Patty Jo's mom was a reporter for the local paper and was granted an exclusive interview. Everyone read her article, which reported that the men were "very polite" but were clearly not from "around these parts." Little did she know some of them were really not from around these parts—like not even from our planet. Anyway, a story about men in suits staking out the local middle school caught attention and spread to the state and even national news. That's when more government types descended.

Turns out that when the Senate Select Government-Alien Joint Task Force Cooperation Council—I'm sure they had a more tortured acronym of a name, but it was super classified, so we never found it out—showed up in our town, they expected to follow the signals of the Rubik's Cubes to an exclusive university, or maybe a Mensa Society convention. Because the government planted the alien tech in Rubik's Cubes to track down certain types of people. When they found an entire middle school instead, they were baffled. Why did every kid in our school seem to be solving Rubik's cubes? Emily had thrown off their algorithm.

The aliens were helping the government look for people with the tenacity to solve impossible puzzles. The aliens weren't supposed to supply tech to our governments, but they were as terrified of mutually-assured destruction as the rest of us. Someone came up with the idea to find and groom some problem-solvers from all over the world who might come up with better ideas for the future.

Of course, at the time, we didn't know about the alien involvement, and we couldn't figure out how they knew about the Rubik's Cubes in our school. (We kids all suspected Jason of snitching to someone.) The government reps quashed the national story and most people never knew what had almost gotten out. But Emily, well, she got recruited to the program. And surprisingly, Patty Jo, Jason, and I got invited along as well.

Now that the news has broken for real, I get to tell you how it was almost revealed all those years ago. And you can ignore those fear-mongering tales about aliens among us trying to do us harm. The truth is, you probably know a few aliens yourself. You just didn't realize it, because they look just like us.

THE WIND AND THE WATER

M. C. SORENSON

I am Jindao, and this is the tale of a cursed forest, a phantom medallion, and the dangerous and alluring thief who would one day steal my heart, but not before nearly stealing my life. It begins in the city of Bugen, in the Valley of Falling Stars, in the Kingdom of Shoshan.

It began on a day when the stars were falling less, and the rain more…much more. The streets of Bugen ran deep with water, leaving only mounted horsemen and wagon drivers free of sodden boots and leggings. My own had suffered hours of wandering, with the rain having soaked through my clothes and causing me more misery than I wished to endure. All in the effort to find the dwelling of Hoi Dupo, an elusive and infamous scribe of arcane writings; the kind of writings that were forbidden by the emperor.

Ahead of me stood a large public house, an establishment of strong drink, food and loud voices. Markings above the courtyard gate denoted it was also a place of rest. At the door a group of people climbed down from a sheltered wagon. The finery of their clothing was lost in the drenching rain, but I could see well enough that they weren't peasant farmers, or day laborers.

I myself was a man who was of a class elevated above the brothers of the earth, but not so much so that I could walk unchallenged among the wealthier societies. I was a servant to Lord Tan Ju, duty bound to serve at his behest, with the rights and privileges accorded such a rank. As such, while I might, upon occasion, be given liberty to council my lord, I would never break bread at his table.

Leaving my misery upon the watery byway, I entered into the house to find food and sleep. I found both; albeit, while the food was filling and well seasoned and the drink refreshing, the lodging was scarce, as all the rooms were filled. The innkeeper, a small man by the name of Wu Sho, apologized profusely at the inconvenience, then showed me to a small sleeping cupboard sufficient for my needs.

That night, after drying my boots and clothing by the fire, I retired to my nook and fell into the sleep of the weary.

It was at the hour of haunting, when all good people slumbered, that I awoke to voices. Not the disembodied kind, which I normally sought to avoid, but the voices of two men talking in low tones, so as not to be overheard. With great care, I silently slid my cupboard door open to better glean their words.

There was much that I could not discern; however, the name Hoi Dupo came easily to my ears. Another one, Huum Jiao, was also known to me. He was a man that bartered in things that were less tangible than what could be found in a market stall. I don't mean to say that he was a thief, or one of those who dealt in human misery; nay, his talent lay in arranging meetings between those who did not wish to be seen together in the light of day.

The men finished their discussion with some mention of enchanted writings, and of gaining Hoi Dupo's service, but they did not divulge their intent. As they left the room to its silence, I lay thinking of their words.

I was fortunate to have overheard their discussion and absently wondered what their purpose may be. Finding Huum Jiao would not be difficult, as he was known in the city among a certain folk. The difficulty would lie in convincing him to arrange an audience with the elusive Hoi Dupo.

It was with this thought, and that of my errand, that I slumbered off again.

The next day found itself cold and damp, with the sky having lowered itself to the ground in a shroud of thick, gray fog. The streets of Bugen, while not pooled with water, were soggy with the remains of the storm's bounty.

I had lingered that morning to witness the coming of the day, as well as to enjoy the brief respite of a warm meal and dry clothing. As such, it was not until the sun had done its duty in bringing a pale light to the world, that I left to seek Huum Jiao.

I found him, just past midday, lodging in one of his many places of seclusion. It had not been a frugal task, having lightened my financial burden by a goodly sum, but I counted myself fortunate the cost was in copper, and not silver.

I found him to be slight of build, but tall, and he carried himself in a manner that spoke of a certain bored nobility. Perhaps it was an act, merely a way to put me at ease while we spoke of business.

"I find it unusual that a servant of the High Lord Tan Ju would find his way to my humble home," spoke Huum Jiao, as he lounged in a chair carved from some exotic dark wood. "Won't he be troubled by such a meeting?"

"Perhaps," I replied. "However, my master does recognize that such things are needful."

"I see. What is it you seek from me?"

"There is in the city, a man, whose knowledge of the art of calligraphy is rumored to be unequaled. I seek an audience with this man, so that I may beg a favor that only he is able to fulfill."

"Indeed," replied Huum Jiao. "And if this master scribe is available, of what value is it to you?"

"I am prepared to pay a goodly sum of silver, provided the meeting is arranged in an expeditious manner."

Huum Jiao paused as he touched his chin with his finger.

"Have you a token, or some such proof that I may show this man? Something that would assure his interest in meeting with you?"

I had such a token, one that would entail great danger if were to fall into the possession of the emperor's agents; however, the risk of discovery by Huum Jiao might result in nothing more than idle curiosity on his part. Judging that his reputation, and his future business prospects were of greater value to himself than illicit information, I handed over a piece of paper, folded and sealed with cord and wax.

"I believe a cost of ten silver moons would place you in this man's company by the end of the day," He said, as he slipped the packet into his robe. "What he would charge, I don't know, but of course you would be free of any obligation, save for a deposit of three moons, if he declines."

"That is acceptable," I replied, as I gave him three silver coins. "I'll expect word at the public house run by Wu Sho."

"Of course."

And with that, I left Huum Jiao's presence, and returned to the inn to spend the afternoon in anticipation of the meeting.

The messenger arrived at evening when the veil of twilight had fallen upon the city. He entered the public house and slipped easily through the crowded common room. The scant light of the guttering oil lamps, and the hood he wore did much to mask his features from casual glances.

"The meeting has been arranged," he spoke quietly. "If it is acceptable, I am to guide you to the dwelling of he whom you seek."

I nodded, and with my belongings, which were few, I followed.

He led me through the darkening streets, turning here, and there, perhaps in an attempt to disorient me, or more likely, to evade anyone who might be in pursuit. Above me, the westerly wind scattered the remains of the storm, revealing the deep purple of the coming night as it cast away the shroud of blue that hid so well the beauties of the heavens.

Presently, we came to a large warehouse crafted of wood and stone, and topped with the tile roof common to this region. It sat centered in a walled courtyard, that at this time held wagons. No animals were present, perhaps having been moved to pasture, or let out for profit.

We entered the building and found an open structure, with the main floor used for the preparation and packing of product. Heavy post and beam construction held up a roof, while a balcony wrapped around the inside of the building, creating lofts for storage. Upon this upper loft, at the rear of the building, were rooms used for the housing of the owner and his employees. Hanging from the heavy ceiling trusses were ropes, wooden pulleys, and stout nets.

Huum Jiao was present with four other men, three of whom I knew to be his bodyguards, having seen them at his residence and recognizing the type. The other appeared in the garb of a student, or perhaps, a disciple. He seemed disinclined to communicate openly with Huum Jiao, and as such, I presumed he served Hoi Dupo.

Huum Jiao and I greeted each other, both bowing in respect and courtesy. I passed the remaining payment to him, and he introduced me to the lone man.

"This is Kio, Master Dupo's assistant. He will escort you."

"My thanks, Master Jiao," I said.

With another bow, he left, his men following.

I turned to the acolyte, who bade me follow him to a corner of the building where we ascended a stairwell to the second level.

"Master Hoi is not a man of many words," spoke Kio quietly, as he led me to one of the rooms. "I was moderately surprised when he acquiesced to meeting with you, as he has not been so accommodating in the past to similar requests."

"I presumed that this was his livelihood," I replied, with some confusion.

"Oh, it is; however, he most often uses a trusted intermediary, such as myself, to broker the actual exchange. This is unusual. I ask you to keep this in mind."

"Of course. I mean no offense at the intrusion."

"No, no, of course not," he reassured me.

As we reached the door, he tapped lightly on it. A voice answered.

Kio slid the door open to reveal a room lit with lamps. To one side was a modest bed with a blanket and cushion. A travel satchel sat at the foot. In the middle of the room stood a table, with a chair occupied by an older man bundled in silk and woolens. At his feet sat a fire bowl filled with hot coals to ease the occasional draft. Upon the table lay paper accompanied by an ink stone, a brush, and a few other items necessary to the art of calligraphy.

"Please, enter," he said, in a voice not used to speaking. "I have been waiting."

I did so, and the door slid shut behind me. I heard the faint shuffling of feet as Kio left us to our business.

"I am most grateful to be allowed to meet with you, honored master," I said. "I am told it is a rare opportunity."

"Ah, not so rare as you might think," he replied. "Once, I used to know many people, and even had the ear of our illustrious nobility, but now I am an outcast. But, I do not wish to bore you with my troubles, instead, I am anxious to know of your request. The token you provided is most intriguing. It is something I have not seen written, save by myself, for many years."

"It is my own clumsy hand that made the stroke," I admitted.

"The calligraphy of Yan Bo Ga is not well known," spoke Hoi Dupo. "Nor is it permitted; not within the borders of this land."

"I would not scribe it, nor have it scribed by any hand, save that there is no other way to achieve my aims," I replied.

Hoi Dupo said nothing for a moment, but then spoke in a quiet tone.

"Are you willing to risk your freedom, even your life, for this?"

"I am."

Hoi Dupo nodded his head in understanding.

"Not only is the calligraphy of Yan Bo Ga rare," he spoke, after a moment, "But it is of a tongue that has been known only among the Shin Wu, that order of monks who bartered in the secrets of royalty, and who are now many years since destroyed."

The look he gave me as he spoke the words meant more than what he had just said, but I said nothing in reply, and he gave only a tight smile in return. After a moment, he took a sheet of paper, replenished his ink stone, and took up a brush.

"Speak what you would have me write."

Now, what I would have him write was an incantation, or words of awakening, in which whatsoever thing it was written on, would, when the words were spoken again, be imbued with a form of life, in the which it would guide the seeker to the item that was sought. This spell I spoke to him as he copied it upon the paper. As he did so, I marveled at his command of the art, for his mastery was beyond any that I had before seen.

When he finished, he set aside his brush, and bade me speak the name of that thing which I sought. I did so, and immediately the paper rustled of its own accord, then lay still. He reached for a bowl, from which he took a measure of fine powder and sprinkled it over the paper. We sat in silence, allowing a moment for the pounce to absorb whatever ink lay undried.

At that moment, I heard from outside the room, the creaking of the floor. I thought that perhaps the acolyte had returned, and wondered how he knew that our business had been completed. But then I heard the scraping of steel upon leather. I snatched the paper from the table, leaving a bag of silver in its place and dodging away just as the door burst apart.

In entered a giant of a man, clad in a leather jerkin, and wielding a battle mace; a four flanged bar of steel with a tapered point. It was better known in the northern provinces, and was designed for crushing blows, but was wielded in the same manner as a large battle sword.

Shoving the finished verse into my tunic, I ducked as the giant swung his weapon. Hoi Dupo, who moved quickly for an old man, snatched what he could from the table and ducked through a hidden door at the rear of the chamber. Leaping into the air, I slammed both feet into my attacker's chest and knocked him back through the door. As he stumbled out onto the balcony, and before he could regain his footing, I struck him with a double kick, which sent him over the railing to the floor below.

Something flicked near me, and I instinctively dodged away. It was a dart trailing a thin tassel. A second whispered by, but my fortune was strong, as it found the wall rather than my flesh. I looked for the attacker, and saw a man obscured by shadow on the opposite side of the warehouse. He raised his arm, and cast another. I moved quickly to my right to avoid the missile, but was suddenly confronted by another darkly clad figure with a snake chain, the preferred weapon of the Do Ba monks.

He was fast, the length of iron links snapping at my head. I avoided the strike, yet barely. Another dart hit where I had been but a moment before, to be followed by the snake chain, with its needle points striking out once more. This time I was less fortunate, and it pierced my tunic sleeve, but with little harm, save for a scratch. The monk shouted for more darts. Having avoided them up until now through luck, rather than skill, I reached for one of my few possessions, and drew it forth.

It was a short sword, with the blade nearly the length of my arm, single edged, and four fingers wide, making it suitable for many things, including defense. It was also light and fast, perfect for deflecting darts, and other weapons of death.

Heeding the monk's words, the dart master cast another two projectiles at me. In the dim light I managed to deflect both. One tacked itself into a post, while the other found purchase in the shoulder of the Do Ba monk.

He held tightly to his weapon, but his arm became useless, leaving me with only one, possibly two, opponents. This problem I quickly addressed by pulling two of the darts from the wall, and throwing them back at the dart master. Whether he dodged them or not, I didn't know, for I flung myself from the loft, my hand grasping one of the ropes that held the hanging nets, and slid to the floor.

The door to the warehouse lay open, the night breeze entering in. I sped towards it, deflecting another deadly projectile in my run, and…

…then she was there, striking from the shadows, her blade similar in size to mine, but more slender and double edged. I parried, and she struck again. Another parry, our eyes met and…I knew her. She slapped my blade with hers, then fled into the night, with something fluttering in her hand. I felt in my tunic for the paper, but it was conspicuously absent. How did she…?

A sound behind me told me the giant had survived his fall. Without a glance, I rushed for the door. The sound of a grunt, the kind that punctuates a great physical effort, caused me to drop to the floor and slide, as the mace, thrown in the manner of a javelin, struck the night air in place of my flesh.

I searched for my female assailant, Mei Xien, for I knew her name, and had crossed her path more than once. The gate was open, but as the wind coursed through the courtyard, I surmised that her method of escape would not lay in that direction. I knew some of her methods, just as she knew of mine, and for this reason, I knew she would seek the quickest route.

I looked to the roof tops.

The city had fallen into the shroud of night, its byways having become rivers of paper lanterns that flowed with the current of people as they moved among each other. The air was chill, for autumn was upon us, with the previous day's storm being the first of many.

Above them, my feet touched the roof tops, but only enough to propel me upon the paths of the wind. For this was a skill which my first master, one who had been Shin Wu, yet had later repented of his error, taught me with his last strength. How Mei Xien had learned this, I knew not, for there were many who had acquired this same talent through the ages.

As I was quick to follow her path, it was not long before I caught sight of her. She was nimble, and sought to evade me, but I was able to match her attempts. It was after these many efforts, in which she tried to lose me, that she resorted to more active measures. Darts and bladed stars were the first weapons she used to discourage me, but these I dodged, or parried away with my blade.

As our course took us further from the center of Bugen, the light grew dimmer, for the people and their lamps were few and scattered. It was here, in this puzzle of shrouded roof tops and dark alleys, that Mei Xien used her most effective defense; one in which she had learned to harness the elements of fire and smoke. It was these ingredients, contained within orbs of paper, and thrown with speed and power, that exploded before me. How many she used, I did not know, but it was sufficient to obscure my vision and to cause me to tumble over a roof, and fall to the ground below.

As I quickly collected myself, and flew back to the roof in an attempt to follow her, I thought I heard laughter. Perhaps it was merely the wind, or my own memories of Mei Xien echoing from the past, but whatever the case, she had disappeared, and I knew not where to seek her.

What I heard next, however, could not be mistaken for either. For it was the voice of a man, a voice I had heard only the night before.

"Quit this errand while you yet live, for what you seek is not for you, nor your master."

Alarmed, I looked about me, yet I could see no one, as night had fully cloaked the neighborhood. Nor was there another sound, save for the wind.

My shame at losing the paper, and thus the means by which to accomplish my mission, weighed heavily upon me. Yet I persisted, despite the warning, for my task was not some trifle that my Lord Tan Ju toyed with for his amusement.

For I sought a talisman that would allow the user to see deeply into the soul of another. Of this object there was much legend, and little truth, for the device was elusive due to the magic with which it was bound. It could only be found through arcane means, hence the need for the verse, and the paper on which it was written.

What is more, this magic was of a type used by the Shin Wu. Now, my master knew that I had some knowledge of it, which I had learned from one who had belonged to that creed. As such, he sent me to find, and bring him, this talisman of power.

He also knew that the Shin Wu were hated by many, if not all, for they had done much to usurp the kingdom and to bring it into chaos. This they did in order that they might establish themselves as rulers. Yet, they were destroyed, and those who had been scattered were hunted and killed. For this reason I kept my past and knowledge hidden, even to where I had adopted, among other things, a different style of fighting.

My master, despite my rejection of the ways of the Shin Wu, also feared this knowledge becoming common among his people. As such, in order to protect me, he tasked me to work alone.

Now, it had been some days since I had left the city of Bugen and had set out to hunt down those who had taken the paper. Obtaining a duplicate was futile, as Hoi Dupo had departed Bugen in haste, and my efforts in finding him would be in vain. As to his acolyte Kio, I knew not of his fate, for he was absent during the fight. Because of this, I presumed he had some part to play in this group of thieves. As to whether I would ever encounter him again, I could only guess.

But, I digress; for this knowledge I did have: I knew of the location, or generally so, of the talisman. For it lay at the heart of a forest, which had spread itself abroad in a valley of whispering stones. Of this place my first master knew, for he had been there, and had heard the voices speak to him.

This valley I now traversed. The forest, with the yellow leaves of autumn carpeting the floor, and with others yet to fall, lay silent, save for the rustling of the canopy in the wind. The whisperings of the stones I had yet to hear, but I did not doubt my master, for his experience had compelled him upon a different path. One which had led away from the Shin Wu.

I traveled no road, as there was none, for it was a haunted place and avoided by all, save for the brave, or perhaps just foolish. This last thought was for myself. Though I did not consider myself a fool, there were times when courage and foolishness were the same. Regardless, at the journey's end I would know, for either I would have obtained the treasure, or I would be dead.

Over rock and rill I went, my feet carrying me forth to my destination. I made no sound save for my gentle breathing and soft footfalls, yet I feared discovery, for none could travel through a forest as a ghost. But I soon encountered the one who came very near to do so.

It was Mei Xien, and she met me with an arrow, my only warning being the slight brush of its fletching upon a leaf. Despite this, if she had meant me to die, I would have. As such, the shaft buried itself in the trunk of a tree.

"Can you not heed a warning?" she called through the canopy. "Do you not know how near you are to meeting your fate?"

"What fate is that?" came my reply, as I ducked into a cluster of trees, hoping to obscure her aim.

"Death, and then oblivion."

"Do not heroes enter into paradise?" I jested.

"Only the brave ones, not the foolish," said she, as her shadow slipped through the golden foliage.

"And what of duty to my lord?"

"It is for fools, for who knows his duty save what Heaven decrees?"

"And what has Heaven decreed for you," I asked, as I drew my blade, and then dashed out of cover and caught the wind into the higher canopy.

"Nothing," she answered, as she let loose another arrow, which I deflected. "For I am untamed by any master, save for what mortality demands of me."

"Nay, for you serve one now, how else are you here?"

She laughed.

"Well said, for you speak the truth; but it is of little matter, for this servitude is but a moment, and is based upon coinage, not bondage."

I caught a glimpse of her as she moved among the limbs, her body lithe, her hair streaming dark behind her, following the currents of the air, as I was. For a moment I could say nothing, but could only feel the beating of my heart, and that brief moment when it skipped. For she was as the wind, forever moving at her own whim, serving none but whom she chose, having nothing, for she needed nothing.

And what was I? Not the wind. Nay, I was as water, flowing within those bounds set for me, or at times resting upon the quiet shore. On those rare occasions, flying as a spirit upon high, to be caressed and teased by the wind, to play, to be something else, but then, fated to fall again upon the earth, to nurture, to serve, and sometimes, to destroy.

"Do you know what your employer seeks?" I asked.

"Must I?"

"Always, for how else do you know if the life you take is worthy of the treasure you seek?"

She said nothing, and for a time we pursued each other in silence through the natural arbor the towering trees provided. I thought perhaps she would tire of this, and wondered at her purpose. To waylay me was a foregone conclusion, but to slay me? I doubted it, for even though her reputation spoke of it, she did not have the coldness of spirit for one who killed for gold.

At length, we arrived at a small, stony clearing, treeless and strewn over with wild vines. Here we paused in our chase, and gazed upon each other from atop the trees on either side of the clearing, the limbs beneath our feet swaying in the wind. For a moment, time seemed bound. But only for a moment, for a rush of air cast a curtain of golden leaves through the void, obscuring for a brief instant, the huntress of these golden woods.

The arrow came, sure and quick, as I knew it must; for although my words were sure to weigh heavy on her heart, her duty, though she denied it, held her bound to her errand. I deflected it easily, but my error was revealed too late, for the head was not of iron, but of paper, and elemental powder.

The smoke took but moments to blow away on the wind, but alas, I found myself upon the ground, my joints in pain from the many branches I had encountered in my fall. Around me stood those thugs from whom I had escaped in Bugen. Their faces were hard, and their eyes cold, save for the giant, who smiled happily as he sent me into unconsciousness with his boot.

"I would have had you killed, save that these words are unknown to me," spoke a voice through the haze in my head. "Speak them, and your life shall be spared."

Before me stood Rin Ho Ja, the man I had overheard speaking in the public house in Bugen, and who had also warned me to abandon my errand while on the rooftops. What his purpose was, I knew not, only that we both sought the same object of power. Beyond this, his manner spoke of strength and cunning, his clothes indicated wealth, and his weapon, the long, double edged blade of royalty, implied command of life and death.

But more so, there were things about him that seemed familiar. Not his physical person, but rather, there were aspects about him that caused me to believe he was Shin Wu. Yet, he spoke not the tongue, nor could read the writing of Yan Bo Ga. Because of this, I was unsure.

Nor did I believe his words of mercy, for his voice was too at ease for such honesty. As such, I would not recite the verses, nay, not until I could secure my life. For I knew more of this secret than he did, and with this knowledge, I would play at his game.

"What would you gain at my words?" I asked, as I tried my bonds, which were well secured.

"I would gain the treasure," he replied. "And you, your life."

"What treasure? An empty box with the remains of burrowing insects within? Perhaps a tomb, vacant, save for the smell of centuries old death mingled among the dry bones of a forgotten king? Or a broken and fallen shrine, washed clean by the rains of a thousand storms?"

"I did not command you to speak in riddles," he said. "What more secrets do you hold?"

"Many, but only one, beyond the verse you wish me speak, which concerns us," I replied. "Did you think the talisman would come so easily to one who dwells solely within this mortal realm? The talisman of Fung Xiao is not so easily discovered through the natural vision, for it is hidden, not merely in this plane of flesh and stone, but in another world into which we may not peer, save for those moments in which magic allows a glance. It is only through the recitation of a second spell that one might obtain it."

Now this object, or medallion, for so I understood it to be such, was first conceived and used by one Fung Xiao, a wizard of ancient time and place as spoken of in the legends. For it was through his wisdom, and his desire to strengthen his realm, that he wrought this object of magic. And for many ages it passed from one ruler to another, but in secret, so that its existence might be preserved from others who would seek it for their own use.

And its power was that of truth and discernment, and was meant to give advantage to the one who would wield it. And its intent was such, that those who would speak lies would be discovered, and those who sought harm would be thwarted, while those whose anger was kindled might be put at ease through words of reason and wisdom.

All this was spoken of in the legends, but not all was remembered. For many small things were lost with each telling, in that only hints and shadows remained of the true nature of this talisman.

"And you know this spell?" asked Rin Ho Ja.

"I do, but I will not speak it, save that I come with you."

"You don't trust my word?"

"Power makes promises worthless," I replied.

"You seek advantage of us," spoke the Do Ba monk, and then to his master. "We must slay him and trust to fortune. For how elusive can this thing be? Is it not here in this valley? Does it not sit at its very center? Surely, we can seek and find such a simple place."

"Fool," answered Rin Ho Ja. "Are the kings of old so foolish as to leave a treasure where a child may find it? Would you have us spend our days searching seam and crevasse for glinting gold or silver? Magic causes stone to move of its own accord, for rivers to change their courses, and trees to part their roots, all this so that thieves may be hindered in their search. Nay, for this man already has us at a disadvantage, for he knows both secrets."

This last he spoke as he commenced bartering with me.

"I will grant you life, for now, but you must honor your part."

"Loosen my bonds," I said. "For what harm can I do, for you are five, and I but one. More so, I am wounded from my fall, and the giant keeps my blade from me."

A moment passed, and whispers of distrust passed between the thugs, but Rin Ho Ja said nothing. Mei Xien stayed silent as well, for she would act upon her own counsel.

"Your bonds will be loosed," Spoke Rin Ho Ja. "But, do not think that you have freedom, for Mei Xien will guard your every move, and counter whatever treachery you may devise."

Upon this I agreed, and my bonds were released.

"Now, speak the words," he said, as he held the paper in both his hands.

With a deep breath, I recited the verse, speaking each word with precision, such as one would a chant a mantra while at worship in a temple. As I finished, the paper rustled a moment in the wind, then lay still. A moment passed as I savored the scent of the forest, for it might be my last. The Do Ba monk grumbled, the giant's feet shifted upon the ground, and the dart master's leather scabbards creaked.

Then, of a sudden, the paper twitched, then bowed up, then snapped into the air and floated between us in the breeze. It rippled, flapped, turned one way, then another; a corner folded, the center crumpled, another fold followed by yet another, and another.

When it had finished, it fluttered as a bird in the air before us. All were amazed, but I quickly gathered my thoughts, remembering to speak the name of the talisman. Once spoken, the paper bird flew off.

"Go!" Shouted Rin Ho Ja, as he leapt to the chase. "Follow it!"

And we did so, moving quickly through the forest, leaping over fallen trees, ducking under branches and between trunks;

for the creature, or whatever it might be called, did not waste effort in finding an easy path.

The others moved easily, though not so lithely as Mei Xien, nor as myself, before having fallen from the tree. Yet, move we did, traversing the golden woods with the sun casting longer shadows upon the ground, for it was late in the day.

As time passed, and the day waned, our aches and fatigue set in. I feared that the treasure was still some distance away, and that we might find ourselves searching for it in the dark. It was at this moment, as the wind changed course and brought with it the coolness of evening, that the whispering began.

The monk heard it first, for he cast his eyes about in alarm, and exclaimed that it was a spirit. The other two hirelings laughed, and said it was only the wind. I glanced at Mei Xien, who looked upon me with confusion.

"Know you of this?" she asked.

"Only stories, for I have never visited this place," I said, neglecting to mention the experience of my first master.

"The monk's mind is weak," said Mei Xien.

"Perhaps, but there are many dangers upon the wind, and not all are of this world."

To this, she said nothing, but we continued on.

"It has stopped!" cried the dart master.

"Where?" asked the giant.

"There!"

We all looked and found the paper bird fluttering high above us, near a ledge. Leading down from it were what appeared to be steps. Rin Ho Ja led the way with the dart master and giant following. Both were glancing about and seemed ill at ease. The monk had stopped and was looking at the forest, his eyes wide with fear, and his hands trembling.

"What are the voices telling you to do?" I whispered to the monk when I got close.

He looked at me with wild eyes.

"They are trying to kill you," I whispered, as I sought to unbalance him. "You need to run away."

He made some strange noise, then bounded up the steps after the others. Behind me, Mei Xien gasped. I turned, and found her raising her hand against the sunset as she peered at the distant stones shrouded by the waning sunlight.

"Do they speak to you as well?" I asked.

She looked at me, her breath trembling, yet whether it was from the climb, or from those whisperings upon the wind, I knew not.

"There is nothing," she answered.

"Nay, nothing, but what speaks fear into your mind," I countered. "For I hear them as well, and would heed them, if not for my duty."

She said nothing, but motioned me on.

The way was narrow, and the steps treacherous, for no one was ever meant to come here again. The monk passed quickly by the dart master, nearly pushing him from the stairs, but found trouble with the giant who filled the gap.

"He is insane," I quietly spoke to the dart master. "The voices have riven his soul. He will kill us all."

"You are wrong," he answered. "We are compatriots."

"But the voices do not know friendship. We are in their realm, and they seek our destruction. They will use us to fulfill their desire."

Ahead, the giant and the monk squabbled among themselves. Rin Ho Ja was hidden from sight, as he had gone on ahead. The dart master looked upon his fellows, and I saw doubt cloud his features.

"You need to stop him," I said, hoping that they would fight among themselves.

He nodded slightly, and went to join his brothers. He spoke to them, but whatever words he used were of little comfort, for the monk reacted violently, and lashed out against him. The dart master defended himself, and the giant sought to grab and hold the monk to still him. Alas, in the struggle, the giant lost his footing on the narrow steps, fell, and tumbled down the path. With him came the dart master, both tangled together. I leapt out of the way, and moved to draw Mei Xien with me, but she had been watching, and had already found safety. The two men flew past us, the giant rolling from the path and over a ledge, where he, and my blade, plummeted to the ground some distance below. The dart master smashed his head against a rock, and lay silent with his eyes unblinking, his life-blood pooling on the stone beneath him. I looked up the path, and watched the monk scramble away, his laughter broken and shrill.

We hurried after, and soon found ourselves standing before a dark opening in the rocks. Here stood Rin Ho Ja with his long, double edged blade in hand, and the monk, who moved from rock to rock, with his snake chain ready to strike. They argued, and the monk struck out with his weapon, but the space was small, and Rin Ho Ja skilled. The chain struck nothing but stone, but the long, double edged blade found flesh. The monk slumped to the ground, his breath nothing more than a death rattle, and his blood a growing stain beneath him.

Rin Ho Ja turned to me, and with a the last rays of the setting sun glinting cold in his eyes, he spoke.

"Come, we are near."

For a time, I thought the voices had no effect upon Rin Ho Ja, for his voice betrayed nothing. Yet, as I came near to him, I saw that his eyes were lit with madness. It was that same madness that had, just now, caused three men to die, but it was tempered with a coldness that the other three did not possess.

Within our provisions we carried lamps and firestones, which we used to light the darkness of the corridor beyond the portal. I was compelled to go first, with Mei Xien following behind. Rin Ho Ja came last with his sword drawn, for he trusted neither of us, as his madness had now blinded him to reason.

The way was dark, but not long, and soon we found ourselves within a space created from natural stone, as one slab was thrust against another, even until the sky was blotted out, and a haven of darkness had formed. The floor had at one time been filled, and leveled, but now portions of it had settled, leaving it treacherous to walk upon. In the middle of the floor, dimly lit by our lamps, sat a stone. It was of waist height, but slender, as if its sole purpose were to display some device, or as I suspected, a talisman. Instead, upon it lay the paper bird, the spell complete and its energy spent.

"Now, you will fulfill your contract," spoke Rin Ho Ja. "Say the words that will reveal my treasure."

I paused, glancing at Mei Xien, who watched with shadowed eyes, but whose fingers caressed the hilt of her blade. I looked at Rin Ho Ja, his eyes impatient and burning with an inner fire. My eyes fell to his blade, upon which was etched symbols; the same ones, that at one time, marked the arms of the monks of Shin Wu.

I stepped up to the stone and lifted the paper bird. Underneath, carved into the stone were the words which I was to speak. Rin Ho Ja, if he had seen these, would certainly have killed me, for I knew not these words until now, but only knew of their existence. By this ploy, I had kept myself alive.

I spoke the words and stepped back.

For a moment, nothing happened, but then, the words rippled. A thin circle of blue light appeared, and the air itself opened as if it were a bloom, revealing its treasure within.

Upon the altar lay the talisman. It was round, yet shaped as a flower, with three lobes of precious metals; one of gold, one silver and the other bronze. A black stone, upon which was carved a serpent crest, was set in the center where the three metals were fused together.

"Finally, it is mine."

Rin Ho Ja snatched the medallion from the stone, and held it in his hand as he gazed at it.

"Now, all secrets shall be mine," he said, his voice joyous, yet harsh. Then his joy turned to anger as he spun, his sword flashing up in defense.

"Nay, my secrets you shall not know," growled Mei Xien as she struck with her blade. Rin Ho Ja parried the blow, countered and missed, but thrust forward, forcing her back upon the uneven ground. She stumbled, but caught herself, slipping to her right in an effort to escape his strikes.

"For this, was this treasure hidden; for this, was this place cursed." spoke a voice in my mind, which, until this moment, had only been whispers upon the air.

"This talisman was not meant for battle, but to seek the truth within, for protection, and healing," I said, in a quiet voice. I tried to move, but was held by some power.

"Yet, you mortals mistrust and deceive, and use this device so that you may have power over another."

"There are those who do such things, yet there are others who seek consolation and friendship. Should this thing be lost because of fear? Should we cast away our desire to seek knowledge and wisdom, simply because it may be used for unlawful purposes? Do not the legends speak of those wise ones who healed their realms, as well as those others who, through their own malice, used this talisman to deceive?"

For a moment there was silence, save for the fighting of Rin Ho Ja and Mei Xien.

"Your words are wise, yet, there is uncertainty. Even you doubt your own people." said the voice.

"Yet, we continue, in the hope that we might find a way," I said.

Silence again, but then:

"Your heart is more pure than many we have encountered. We shall hinder you no longer, but go, and do as you will. May this be upon you."

Then the voice left me, while the heaviness that lay upon me ceased, and I stepped forward to battle. For Rin Ho Ja had beaten upon Mei Xien, and had caused her to falter. She lived, but would not much longer. As I moved against him, he turned to strike me. Yet, that secret knowledge, with which I had hidden deep within me, came forth. For though he fought with the skill of a master, I was now certain he knew not the ways of the Shin Wu.

As such, I dodged his blow and struck his arm with my fist, causing his sword to fall to the ground. I struck again, wounding his leg and causing him to stumble to his knees. For a moment he wavered. Then, with his other hand, he whipped out a dagger that had been hidden in his robe, and struck. But the attack was weak, and I countered it and turned his blade. He cursed me and struggled, but I was the stronger one, and with his own hand, I drove it deep into his heart.

For a moment, I saw the madness fade from his eyes, then they passed from life into death as his body slumped to the ground, causing the talisman to fall from his robe. I took it and looked upon it for a moment, then secured it within my tunic.

I turned to Mei Xien, who held her blade towards me.

"What trickery is this, that you may defeat a master swordsman with nothing but your hands?" she demanded. "Have you merely played with me this day? Do you seek my life as well?"

"Nay, Mei Xien, I seek to take nothing from you," I said. "But we must leave this place."

"The whispering…it…," she murmured, then her voice faltered.

"It will trouble you no more, if we go."

She trembled, and I saw that she would faint, for she had lost blood.

"I will care for your wounds." I said.

"They are not deep…" she replied, then, after a moment. "Will you return to serve your master?"

"Yes, for it is my duty."

I reached down and took a purse of coins from Rin Ho Ja's body and held it out to her.

"What you are owed, for you earned it," I said.

She took the leather pouch, and tucked it into her belt. Then, with a painful wince, she sheathed her blade.

"Let us leave," she said.

"I will travel with you, for it is a long journey."

"Not for the wind," she answered, with a crooked smile.

I smiled back.

"Nay, not for the wind."

Jindao will return in the next issue of SFI.
Get your subscription today!

Old City, Eric Wallis. Illustration for Universe, The Sci-Fi RPG published by Tower Ravens, LLC.

As an international student, Jake Dawson finds himself in the middle of a political overthrow. The status quo is challenged, and the seditionists take control of the economic engines of society. Jake defies the shifting landscape, ignores the cancellation of his visa, and remains with his friends to stop the transformation in the land he's come to love.

While he's aware his action may help his friends, he fails to see the drastic change he'll force upon of his own life. His maneuvering will shift not only the landscape of the country, but the history of their entire world.

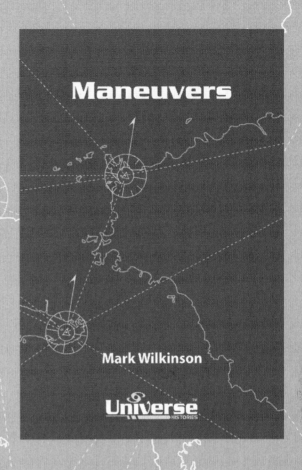

Available now on DriveThru Fiction

Trade Paperback, full-length novel
Paperback or ePub   12 USD
Paperback and ePub   13 USD

https://www.DriveThruFiction.com/product/424547/Maneuvers

Made in the USA
Columbia, SC
14 April 2025